A RING OF TRICKSTERS

Animal Tales from America,
the West Indies, and Africa

This one's for me, Mother Trickster

—V.H.

And for Elizabeth Casey Martin

—B.M.

A RING OF
TRICK

Animal Tales from America, the West Indies, and Africa

THE BLUE SKY PRESS
An Imprint of Scholastic Inc. · New York

STERS

VIRGINIA HAMILTON

Illustrated by

BARRY MOSER

THE BLUE SKY PRESS

For information regarding permission, please write to: Permissions Department, The Blue Sky Press, an imprint of Scholastic Inc., 555 Broadway, New York, New York 10012.
The Blue Sky Press is a registered trademark of Scholastic Inc.
Library of Congress Cataloging-in-Publication Data
Hamilton, Virginia. A ring of tricksters: animal tales from America, the West Indies, and Africa / Virginia Hamilton; illustrated by Barry Moser.
p. cm.
Summary: Eleven trickster tales that show the migration of African culture to America via the West Indies.
ISBN 0-590-47374-3
1. Afro-Americans—Folklore. 2. Trickster—Juvenile literature. 3. Tales—Africa. 4. Tales—West Indies. 5. Tales—Southern States. [1. Afro-Americans—Folklore. 2. Trickster. 3. Folklore—Africa. 4. Folklore—West Indies. 5. Folklore—Southern States.] I. Moser, Barry, ill. II. Title.
PZ8.1.H154Ri 1997 398.2—dc21 96-37543 CIP AC
10 9 8 7 6 5 4 3 2 1 7 8 9/9 0 1 2/0
Printed in Singapore
First printing, November 1, 1997

CONTENTS

THE STORY RING OF TRICKSTER TALES—*A Note from the Author* 9

TRICKSTERS—AMERICAN 13

Buh Rabby and Bruh Gator 15
Buzzard and Wren Have a Race 25
The Cat and the Rat 33
Bruh Wolf and Bruh Rabbit Join Together 39

TRICKSTERS—WEST INDIAN 45

That One, Anansi 47
Magic Anansi 53
Cunnie Anansi Does Some Good 59

TRICKSTERS—AFRICAN 73

Cunnie Rabbit and Spider Make a Match 75
How Chameleon Became a Ride 85
Old Mister Turtle Gets a Whipping 91
The Animals Share 97

ABOUT THESE TALES 105

THE STORY RING OF TRICKSTER TALES

A Note from the Author

A RING OF TRICKSTERS takes us to the time when animals stood tall and walked and talked. It is the story time of those well-known practical jokesters in folklore literature who take advantage of others by playing tricks on them. They are the animal trickers, also known as tricksters. Bruh Rabbit and Anansi, the spider, are the best known of these culture heroes. With other tricksters—Turtle, Lizard, and Wren, for example—they play a variety of roles in folktales from America to Africa. Usually weaker and smaller than most other animals, the animal tricksters are gifted with the power of cunning and, sometimes, magic.

The tales in *A Ring of Tricksters* grew out of a common type of African folktale in which a very human-acting animal uses his wit and cunning to take advantage of bigger and stronger animals. Sometimes this animal will help others, but always, it takes care of itself first. In East Africa, the trickster is Hare and is a rodentlike creature with long ears and long hind legs for leaping. In West Africa, it is Spider or Turtle. More than one of these tricksters can be in a story. And a battle royal may take place to see which animal is the trickiest.

The first African Americans brought trickster tales with them to the southern United States and the Caribbean West Indies. These black peoples also made up new trickster tales of their own, about the kind of animals they encountered in the American South and Jamaica, the Bahamas, and other Caribbean Islands. All of these new tales kept the pattern of the African trickster tales in which a resourceful animal hero having human traits used deceit and sly trickery, and often magic, to get what it needed from bigger and stronger animals.

Another animal trickster crept into the folk patterns of Sierra Leone, on the coast of West Africa. In the colloquial Creole speech, it was called Cunnie Rabbit. Cunnie (cunning) Rabbit was quite small and not a rabbit at all but a tiny "water deerlet," a small gazelle, known for its agility and slyness. It is described by early tale collectors as being about eighteen inches long with little ears, small horns, a soft, fawn-colored coat, dainty legs, and hooved feet. Because it was so swift and nearly impossible to catch, the Sierra Leone peoples thought Cunnie Rabbit had great power and called it "king of the beef for wise," the "beef" meaning all other animals. Where did this shy creature get the name Cunnie Rabbit? And how is it that an occasional "Nancy" (or Anansi) story appeared in Sierra Leone newspapers in the 1860s?

In 1787, Granville Sharp, a British abolitionist, had established on the site that is now Freetown, the capital of Sierra Leone, on the coast of

West Africa, a homeland for freed Africans who had been former slaves in England and had fought in America on the side of the British during the American Revolution. Eventually, former slaves came not only from England to Freetown but from the West Indies and from slave ships captured by the British navy. Their descendants became known as Sierra Leone Creoles, and today they outnumber the Mende and Temne inhabitants who had migrated from interior Africa.

The fascinating ring of trickster tales is like a circle: it began in Africa and moved to America and the Caribbean, and returned again, back to Africa, as former slaves returned to the homeland and brought with them their stories from the new world. It's possible that this is one way some of these tricksters might have crossed the ocean.

In *A Ring of Tricksters*, I present the very best of these exciting, timeless tales. For the benefit of the Global Village and all of its children, let us hope that the story ring will remain forever unbroken.

TRICKSTERS—AMERICAN

THE FIRST AFRICAN AMERICANS told new tales that grew out of the conditions they found in the American South. Their insights into their surroundings gave rise to a unique form of the animal trickster tale. With their keen observations, these early Americans imbued the trickster tale with a finely tuned understanding of their new world and those in it who had power over them.

They learned what justice was, and they learned, as slaves, they had none. But they were able to make up stories and even laugh in the face of their tragic predicament. Thus, they gave the animal tricksters exaggerated human characteristics and comical, entertaining tricks to play.

The best-known animal trickster is Bruh Rabbit, who has been called at different times Brer Rabbit, Brother Rabbit, Buh Rabby, Bo Rabby, B'Rabby, and Son Bunny. Bruh Rabbit is smart and clever enough to escape most any trap. Although small and not very strong, he is secretly cunning. Bruh Rabbit is the emblem and culture hero who symbolizes freedom for all those held in bondage.

The tales in this section acquaint us with not only the antics and exploits of Bruh Rabbit, but also with Wren and Fox and others. They all use their wits to get the better of creatures who are usually larger and stronger. Moreover, these animal trickster tales demonstrate the abiding faith and confidence early African Americans had in themselves, and their remarkable storytelling abilities.

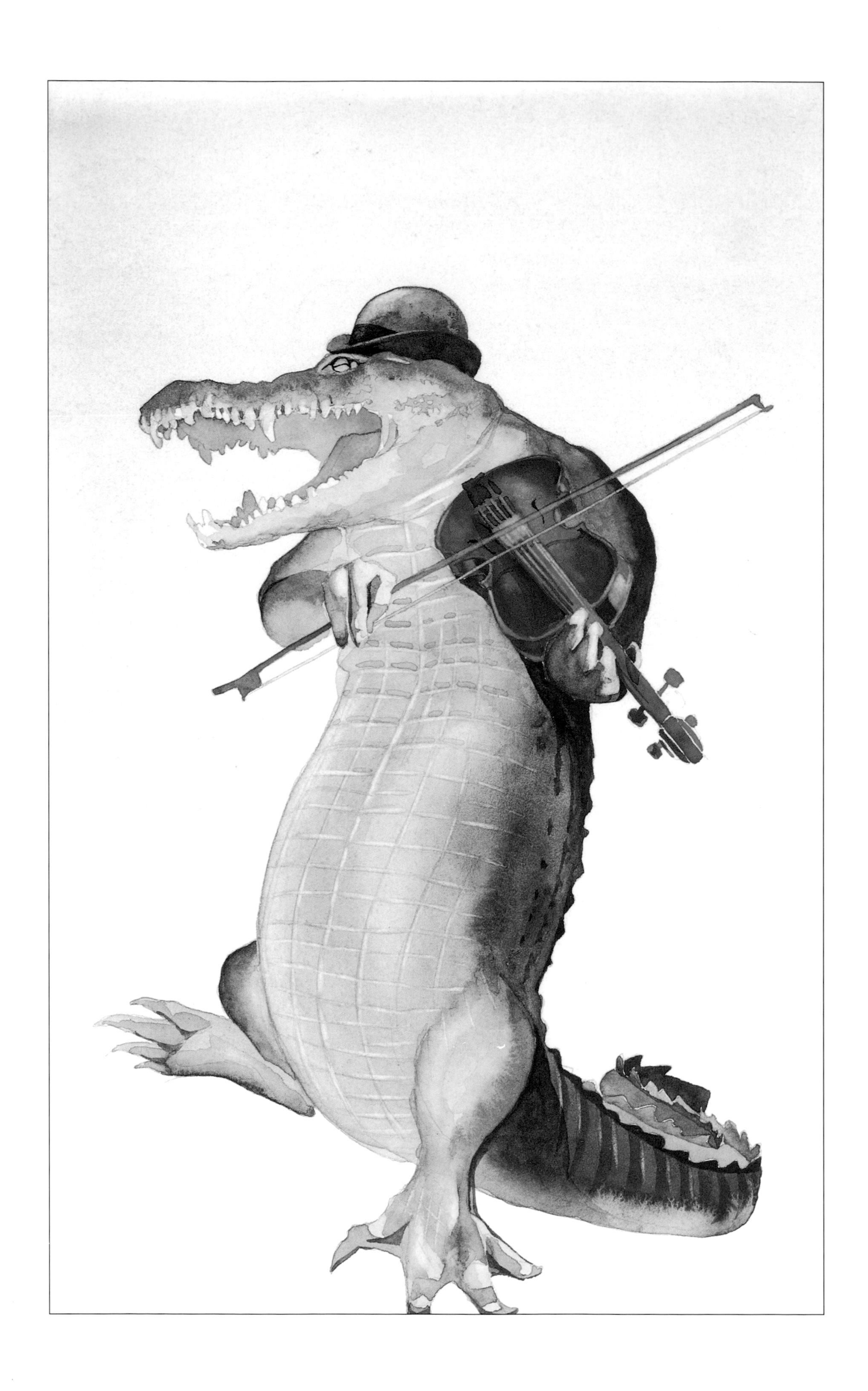

BUH RABBY AND BRUH GATOR

OH, YES! OH, MY! Buh Rabby is a cottontail, for true! And played a trick on rough-skin Bruh Gator one time.

They call Bruh Gator the fiddler. "*Fiddle-faddle fiddle-dee-dum.*" He's the music man. He plays at the dances for the gator girls and boys. He hollers the calls:

"Hold the hands this-a-way!
Bow and say,
'Twirl me round!'
Turn your partner, make a sound!
Whoopee-some!
And take your partner home."

One dance-in, the gator children were having themselves a good, slam-tail, sway-back time. Bruh Gator was playing fine on his fiddle. "Every day is good," said he. "I have no pincher in my life." He meant, he didn't know any kind of trouble. He didn't even know what trouble was. No, sir, he didn't.

That cottontail rabbit, Buh Rabby, marched inside the gator's house, ready to hop-to-dance.

"Halt!" Bruh Gator shouted. "No bunnies dancing in here. *I* dance in here. This is a *gator* house!"

Bruh Gator stood up on the very tip of his tail. Then, he slid down and whipped that tail around. Knocked Buh Rabby clean out of the house with it. The whole time, Bruh Gator never quit dancing or playing his fiddle.

Buh Rabby's head hit the ground before his feet did. Pained him hard! But he didn't let on that his feelings were hurt, too.

He grinned all under his whiskers and called out, "Bruh, you are a dancing gator, for true." Rabby stood there outside the dance, just looking in. He called again to Bruh Gator, "Oh, my, gator-boy, you take a rest. I'll fiddle; I'll take over while you catch your breath."

Bruh Gator was winded, for true. He wiped his brow and said to all the gators, "We'll let Buh Rabby try his hand. He'll be tired in a minute, and I'll take over and kick him out again."

Bruh Gator handed Rabby the fiddle. The rabbit took it up and played. He sang so sweet:

"*Some day good,*
oh, some day!
Some day bad,
how sad!
Today, the music
suits you gators.
I'm most glad!"

He fiddled his way clear through the melody to the last note. Gator boys and girls looked, and they warmed to Buh Rabby's tune. After three more tunes, Buh Rabby had the whole house dancing up a storm.

Bruh Gator didn't like that one bit. He was so upset, he rushed out of there. He waddled over to the big pond and slid himself down in it. "Some day bad," he moaned.

Buh Rabby came out, heard him, and found him there. "What's that you said, my friend?" he called to Bruh Gator.

"Said that I am in deep," Bruh Gator answered.

"You mean, you are in trouble," said Buh Rabby.

"What is that? What is trouble?" asked the gator. He'd never heard of trouble, no way, anyhow. But he thought to say to the rabbit, "Give me back my fiddle."

"I'll give it back, but you don't want it while you're in the pond," said Buh Rabby. "Come on out and dance to a tune I got."

Rabby started to play:

"*Bin-dilly station*
bang-a-lang-a.
Lin-binny station
bang-a-lang-ahh."

It was a fine tune, and Bruh Gator slid on out of the pond.

"Come on, dance it," Buh Rabby urged him. "Dance your big ole tail dance. An'en, slide down, go 'tween my hind feet real fast, and come back slow."

Bruh Gator was 'tween a rock and a hard place and didn't know it.

Buh Rabby did. To himself he said, "I'm a-going to get you, Bruh Gator. You treated me wrong!"

As the gator danced and slid and came back slow, Rabby jumped on his head. Knocked Bruh Gator out clear to sleeping.

He did!

Bruh Gator woke up a day later. The dance was over. All the gators were gone. Bruh Gator was the only one left, and what sat beside him? A tall squirrel, wearing round eyeglasses. Squirrel had Bruh Gator's fiddle set under his chin.

"Call me Buh Squinten Squirrel one time," that squirrel told Bruh Gator. He played on the fiddle. Real pretty tune.

"*Humma humma*," Bruh Gator hummed along. "I sure been in some trouble lately."

"How's that?" asked Buh Squinten Squirrel.

"Buh Rabby showed me trouble for true," said the gator. "He pounded my head, made me sleep through the gator dance."

"Well, some day bad," said the squirrel. "There's no accounting for bad bunnies. Come, take on the dance. You'll feel better."

"You think I might?" asked the gator.

"Surely. Just get up on your tail-end," said Squinten Squirrel. "Then dance on 'tween my hind feet real fast, and come back slow."

"You just said something that reminds me of . . . I can't think what," Bruh Gator said.

"Do like I tell you while I fiddle," Squinten Squirrel said.

And he fiddled:

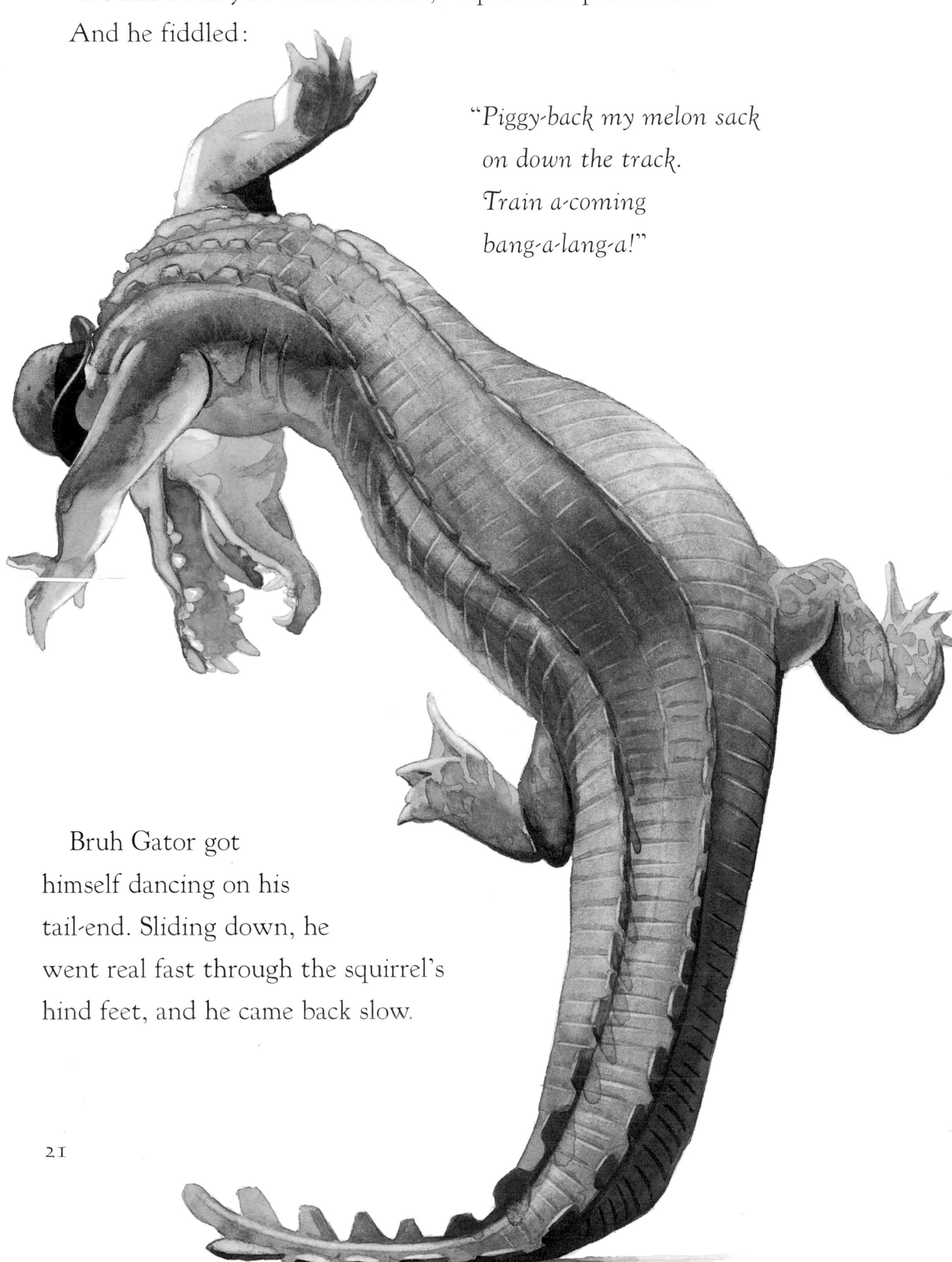

"Piggy-back my melon sack
on down the track.
Train a-coming
bang-a-lang-a!"

Bruh Gator got himself dancing on his tail-end. Sliding down, he went real fast through the squirrel's hind feet, and he came back slow.

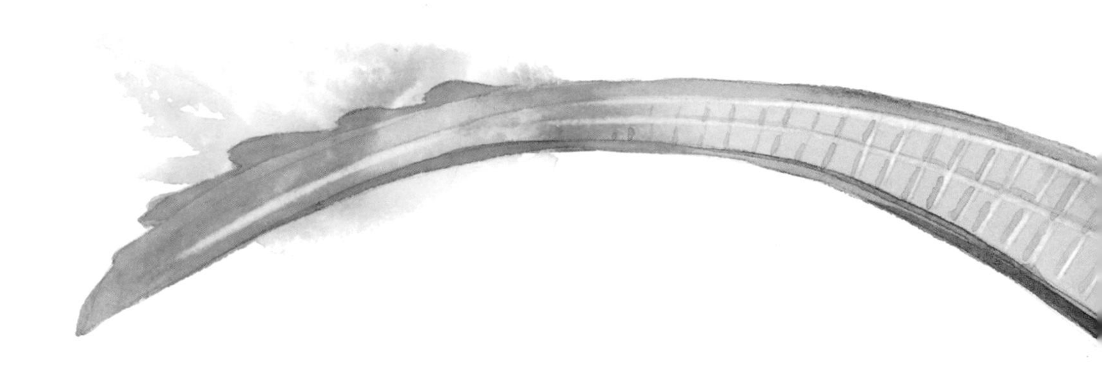

He looked around, and he caught a glimpse of some big, stand-up ears. He saw smoke curling along his tail. Right next, that sometime-squirrel ran off just hee-hawing. And Bruh Gator saw his own whole tail on fire.

"HUMMA! HUMMA!" he shouted. "I'm in trouble again!"

He sure was. For that wasn't any squirrel running off. That was Buh Rabby playing another hard trick on him.

Bruh Gator dived into the pond before his tail was cooked. The tip got singed. He hasn't danced on his tail-end since. And till yet, Bruh Gator has a knot 'tween his eyes and his mouth where that rabbit feet-jumped on him.

Oh, that Rabby, him. He gets even with gators whenever he has a mind to. And forever, gators will try to catch bunnies whenever they can.

BUZZARD AND WREN HAVE A RACE

WAS A TIME, these two breathed the same air. Only, Wren sat his chattering self on the fence rail. And Bruh Buzzard, he soared way high in the sky.

Each could see the other.

Wren could look up and see the buzzard shape against the blue. "Like he's floating in a pool," Wren thought.

Keen-eyed Buzzard could look below from a great height. There he saw Bruh Wren, hard by the meadow, near the fence corner. "No bigger than a mouse, him!" the buzzard thought.

For true, both knew how to fly. It was just that the wren flew lower, and the buzzard flew higher.

And one day, Bruh Buzzard thought he'd have some fun. He

came swooping down to set himself on the fence rail beside Bruh Wren. Scared Bruh Wren half to death at first. But soon, he got used to the mighty wingspan and bald head of Bruh Buzzard. Big him, he was like some heavy shadow come spread over the small likes of Wren.

"You know what?" Bruh Buzzard spoke in a deep, slow squawk.

"Say what?" asked Bruh Wren.

"We are both the same. Except, I'm great big, and you are way little."

"Tell me something I don't know!" chirred Wren.

"Then listen," the buzzard said. "I can do something you can't."

"What's that?" asked Bruh Wren.

"I can fly so high, you can barely tell me from a cloud. And you can't do that."

"You think I can't?" trilled Bruh Wren.

"I know you can't!" hissed Bruh Buzzard.

"All right, Bruh Buzzard. Suppose we have a race!" ticked the wren.

"All right!" the buzzard exclaimed. "Now remember, you have to go as high as I go."

"How could I forget?"

At once Bruh Wren, small as he was, gave out with his ringing, tinkling melody. It was long and beautiful, and the buzzard envied the sound of it.

But not to be outdone, Bruh Buzzard made a show of spreading his massive wings. "You with me, Little Bit?" he asked Bruh Wren, over his shoulder. Couldn't see the little bruh, what with his wings all wide and dark.

"Oh, I'm right with you!" Bruh Wren answered. And so he was. Just as Bruh Buzzard had opened his great wings to fly, Wren

sprang up to rest lightly in the hollow of the buzzard's back.

Bruh Wren went right up with him! They soared!

"Where are you, Bruh?" the buzzard hissed on the air.

"Way high up! I'm right here, Bruh!" Wren called. "Keep going!"

Higher and higher Bruh Buzzard went. His wingtips almost skimmed the sky. Bruh Wren tried to touch the blue but couldn't quite reach it.

"I-yee! I-yee!" called Bruh Buzzard. "Bruh Wren, I can't see you!"

"I-yee! That's 'cause I'm right above you now," trilled the wren. "Come up here with me!"

"No, no, not today," said Bruh Buzzard, afraid the little bruh's wings might get worn out. "We best go back down."

"But it's so nice, flying in and out of clouds," said Bruh Wren.

They sailed comfortably down to the ground. At once, Bruh Wren hopped off his buzzard ride. The two mismatches settled on the corner rail.

Buzzard said, "Bruh? Why is it you never go flying higher than this fence? You can fly as high as me."

Bruh Wren went, "Tic-chir-tic," the way wrens have a mind to do. "If I told you that, you'd know as much as me!" And he gushed a bright, jokey song, as only he knew how to do.

Bruh Buzzard hunched his shoulders. He wondered about it all; yet and still, he kept his hooked beak shut.

THE CAT AND THE RAT

Cat and Rat found a great hard piece of dry old cheese in the cupboard. They carried it away to share it, they did, to eat it up. But they couldn't agree how to divide it.

"I take this half?" asked Bruh Cat.

"No, I take that half, you take this other half," said the rat.

"Maybe I should have more because I'm bigger," said Bruh Cat.

"No, indeed," Rat answered. "Share and share alike is fair, Brother."

"Well, let's get Old Fox to decide," said the cat.

Rat agreed. They called on Bruh Fox. They said, "We want you to be the judge."

"Do you now!" said Fox. "Well, then, I'll bring my scale for to weigh the cheese." And so he did.

Fox put the cheese upon the top of his scale. He examined it carefully. "It don't weigh even," he said. He took out his knife and cut a little piece of it, and he put the piece beside him. "That there little piece is for the judge," he told Cat and Rat. "Now the cheese weighs much better!"

Cat and Rat watched him, and they nodded their heads. They never had seen a cheese weigh-in before. Come to think of it, they never had seen any kind of weigh-in at-all until just then, nor had a judge ever done that work.

Fox leaned his head to one side, then to the other side. He pricked up his ears and let them down again. He showed just some little teeth, but not enough to scare anybody.

"What you be doing?" asked Rat.

Fox shook his head. "This cheese you brought me just don't weigh in right. I'm a-going to put this little piece back and cut another piece for the judge." And so Fox did, a bigger piece this time. He put it beside him. He took the smaller piece and put it back on top of the cheese.

"Now the cheese be weighing more like it's supposed to. See?" asked Bruh Fox.

"That so?" asked Cat.

ACME

"Didn't I just say so?" answered slippery Bruh Fox. He put the cheese back on the scale, and more than half of it was cut away.

Bruh Cat and Bruh Rat stared at one another. How'd that happen? They looked over at Bruh Fox. Looked at the cheese on the scale and the piece set down beside the fox.

"There's been some *subtract* somewhere," said Bruh Cat.

"You saw me *add* that cheese back, now didn't you?" asked Fox.

Still, less than half of the cheese was on the scale. "Hold on, now, Judge! This can't be right," said Bruh Rat.

"You are taking all the cheese! You leave us with hardly none," Bruh Cat complained.

Bruh Fox looked shocked. His fur stood up on his neck. His eyes glinted cold and winter bright.

"I'm taking my scale!" he shouted. He stuck up his thin nose and folded his scale.

He hollered a howl at them: "You bruhs are the bad ones! You go find some cheese and steal it. And you are going

to tell me how to do justice? Better be glad I just-take the cheese and not just-bite your heads off!" Bruh Fox lunged at them. And yipped and barked loud at them. Scared Bruh Cat and Bruh Rat so—they ran off as fast as they could go. Bruh Fox was left with all the cheese. But Cat and Rat, they learned something. They did, for true. What was it?

Finders, keepers; losers, weepers. Never call in a bigger rogue to *add*, *subtract*, and *divide* for you. For there's always *less* than honor among thieves.

BRUH WOLF AND BRUH RABBIT JOIN TOGETHER

NOW'S A NOW, and it's an it. Now, it was yesterday when Old Bruh Wolf and Flop-ears Bruh Rabbit decided to plant a patch of peanuts together. And they did, too, getting along the whole time. One would dig while the other hoed. Wolf pulled weeds, and the rabbit carted away those he didn't find tasty enough to eat.

After a time, sunshine and showers, days and nights, the patch of peanuts peeked aboveground. The two partners waited beside the patch, just resting and watching in the shade.

"Peanuts, showing their green heads," Bruh Rabbit remarked.

"I like that!" Bruh Wolf said, growling with pleasure.

Next time, rain and heat, Bruh Rabbit and Bruh Wolf were

sitting there by the peanut patch. Bruh Rabbit says, "Oh, the tops, the tops! The green peanut tops are coming up!"

And Bruh Wolf thought to say, "Oh, they are so very topping green, too!" If he'd known how to laugh, he would have. He showed his teeth for happiness.

Sun-hot and long, warm nights. Hollered the rabbit one day, "The peanuts are ready, Bruh Wolf! Which part do you want?"

"Huh?" grunted Bruh Wolf.

"I say which, Bruh. Which part of the peanut plant do you want?"

"Oh, well," said Bruh Wolf, thinking hard. (And believe me, thinking was most hard for the big old bruh.) "I don't know which I must take!" he groaned. "I just don't know."

"Tell you what," says Bruh Rabbit. "Let's settle it this way. You take the top. And I'll take the bottom."

"Oh, yes!" cried Wolf. "The green top. I take the top. Oh, yes!"

And so it was that Bruh Wolf had the top, and Bruh Rabbit had the bottom. Bruh Wolf took his green tops home. And Bruh Rabbit shook the soil off the bottoms and carried his home.

"Tomorrow we meet and sell our plantings," Bruh Rabbit said.

And so they did meet, and they went out to market. And Bruh Rabbit called up and down and around, "Peanuts! Peanuts. Fresh, tasty peanuts!"

Old Bruh Wolf was right behind him, almost singing a growl—"Tops! Tops! Fresh green tops!"

Everybody came to see. And Bruh Rabbit sold out all his peanuts, except for the best ones he saved for himself.

And is and, and yet is yet. And Bruh Wolf hasn't sold his green tops yet.

So is so, and next is next. So next came spring, and Bruh Rabbit asked Old Bruh Wolf to go partners. So Wolf told him, he did, "This time, I take the bottoms!"

"All right," said the rabbit. "That's only fair."

"This time, we plant some corn," Bruh Wolf told him.

"All right, Bruh, you got a right to say what kind we planting this time," said the sly rabbit.

And so they did plant corn. The weather was good and hot with rain. And the corn came in, and the morning glories came up in the corn, like they always will. And then it was ready. The two bruhs harvested the corn for selling. Bruh Wolf happily took his part, and Bruh Rabbit took his.

And they went to sell: Rabbit hollering, "Corn! Good fresh, sweet corn for sale!"

And Bruh Wolf right behind him, calling, "Bottoms! Good ole corn bottoms!"

Guess is guess, and who is who. Guess who didn't sell a thing the whole season? Howsomever, maybe Bruh Wolf learned something about a rabbit: Bruh Flop-ears is always asking for help. Then, he helps himself!

TRICKSTERS—WEST INDIAN

IN THE WEST INDIES, there is a certain house spider that has a yellow-striped body and hairy legs. It is said to be harmless but unlucky. And it is called *Anansi*. This word, like many West Indian words, comes from Africa, the ancestral homeland of many West Indians. In the language of the Tshi or Ashanti people on the African West Coast, *Ananse* means spider. The word *nan* means to spin. How easily we spin a spider tale! All Ashanti stories are called *Ananisem*, translated as *story*, whether they are about spiders or not. In Africa, *spider* is the translation for *Ananse*, the animal trickster. In the West Indies, *Anansi* is the name for the spider animal trickster. West Indian *Anansi* stories generally are told to children and elder adults. In this section, we are introduced to *Anansi-tori*. The word is a colloquial expression for *Anansi* story, which many kinds of tales are called. As with *Ananisem*, they may or may not be about spiders. In our *Anansi-tori*, *Anansi* trickster is up to his good or bad, but always magical, tricks. The three tales in this section are written in modified West Indian gullah speech. Gullah grew out of a combination of English, French, Spanish, and African languages at the time of the Plantation Era. The language construction may sound different or strange at first. But by the end of our *Anansi-tori*, it will seem pleasantly familiar.

THAT ONE, ANANSI

TIME WAS, a long time ago, when that one, Anansi, called upon Big Alligator. "I'm out late, Brother," Anansi Spider told him, "and I need a place to sleep the night."

Alligator says, "All right then, come into my house. Stay the night."

Anansi tells Alligator back, "I won't bother you. Sleep me in your house. I want to sleep me in your kitchen."

Telling you, in those days, there be a stone-built kitchen off in the yard. That was what Anansi Spider was thinking about—getting by himself in the kitchen off from Big Alligator's house.

"All right, Brother," Alligator tells Anansi. "You sleep in the kitchen."

Anansi be up to something, for true.

Big Alligator's daughter, Ama, she knows. She's been listening behind the door. Ama hears every word between her father and Anansi-tricker.

At once, Ama goes out and catches one pity-full of scorpions. You know, pity be about two hand-stings, fingers-swelling, full. That's it. Ama takes them, scorpions. Real careful, she! And she puts them in empty kitchen pots. For Ama knows Anansi loves looking in food pots.

Big Alligator slides to the kitchen to say good night. "Well, then," he says, like that, to Brother Anansi.

"Then, too," says Anansi.

"Sleep you sound, then, too, Brother," Big Alligator tells him.

"Well, Brother, I will do that, then, too," says Anansi, yawning.

Telling you, all go quiet, all over the island. Everybody everywhere go to sleep. Palm trees sway a soft rustling—them, they be dreaming so, sweet coconut dreams.

Anansi goes to bed. He lies down until he thinks everybody be sound asleep. Then he gets up, skitters him across the floor, and finds the food pots.

He puts his hand into a pot, knowing he's going to find him something tasty. And he does find it. He knows which are the scorpion pots, and he dare not go reach in them. He eats and eats, all fill-up. He have he-self a good time.

Oh, mahn, that Anansi-tricker! Here's what he does. He's full of food now, and he starts hollering, "Yi-yi!" An'en, he jumps back, sucks his hand, yelling, "Ow-wow-ow!" Like that.

Big Alligator hears him and comes crawling fast. "What it be, Brother Anansi?" Alligator wants to know.

"Brother, I am eaten alive!" yells Anansi. "The fleas here come bitin' me so bad! Your kitchen full of fleas! I got to go!" And rude tricker-mahn, Anansi, scurry out of there.

There be no fleas. There be scorpion, but Anansi be too smart for them.

Ama goes and finds all the eggs gone. She knows who. "Daddy, help!" she cries out. "Anansi eat up all our eggs! All our eggs be inside Anansi Spider!" And Big Alligator runs out after Anansi-tricker.

Heavy Anansi, big eater, he's near the sea by now. On the wharf, he hears Alligator blow his conch shell. "Ahwooo!" Again it goes, "Ahwooo!" And Big Alligator is hollering, *"Stop right there, fella Anansi!"* No Brother Anansi, now, don't-cha-know.

There the boatman comes in his boat, and Anansi tells him, "If you take me across the water, I will give you half my land."

"All right," says the boatman.

Big Alligator is on the wharf. "Stop, fella Anansi!" An'en Big Alligator throws he-self in the water. Too late. He tries, but he can't catch the boat.

When the boat reaches the other side, Anansi leaps upon the land. He says to the boatman, "I'll go tell my father you have come for the land."

The boatman says, "All right, then."

Anansi finds his own father. He tells him that Alligator is after him, and about the boatman. Tells him, "If the boatman or Alligator find you, you say you don't know where Anansi be. Because Brother Anansi is going to climb a tree!"

Finally, the boatman comes. "Where be Brother Anansi?" he asks.

Father says, "I don't know where that one, Anansi, be."

After the boatman goes, Anansi climbs another tree. An'en, Anansi sees Big Alligator coming. As Alligator slides under the tree, Anansi calls, "You see me here, Brother?"

Big Alligator looks. And he looks. So saying, "If I can't find you, fella Anansi, I'll never live in a house again. I'll go live in the water." He looks some more. He find something? Or nothing.

Now you tell me—where does Big Alligator live? You answer me true. An'en, I'll give you . . . my story end!

MAGIC ANANSI

TIME WAS, not so very long ago, when that one, Anansi Spider, had a friend, Him Tiger. And he had another friend, Sana Goat, and all her little kids.

All of them—Anansi, Tiger, and Goat—lived in and about the very same house. That one, Anansi, lived up on top of the roof. Him Tiger lived inside the house. And Sana Goat lived down under the house.

For a long time, they got along together. But one time, Him Tiger had to make a quarrel. Him tell Anansi, "Brother, you make too much dust." Him say to Sana, "Your little kids make too much dirt." Then Him throw back he head and swell he chest, proud, and tell'um, "I want this house to me-self!"

An'en he roared like a b-i-i-i-g tiger. Him scare the little kids so, they scramble back down under the house.

Sana Goat says, "All right, I'll take my kids and go away from here."

And Anansi, he says, "Me, I'm a-get outta here."

Both of them are a-tremble with fear of Big Him Tiger; Him, tongue hanging out and licking his jowls.

Oh, they went fast and faster. And Him Tiger growl, *"Grumma! Grum! Grum!"*

All of them, Brother Anansi, Sana Goat, and the kids, fly in a hurry now. They come to the river. There are a great lot of white stones on the bank of the water. Awful pretty sight, too. Brother Anansi, he fills up with his magic, don't-cha-know. "Hear me now," he tells Sana Goat. "You stand still, and your kids stand still, too."

"All right," she says. And she cautions her kids not to move.

Then brother magic, Anansi, changes Sana and her little ones into smooth white stones. Oh, yes! And brother magic, Anansi, tosses them across the stream to the other side.

The stones whizz over, sparkle in the sunlight. An'en as soon as they touch ground, the stones change into goat and kids again. And the kids just laugh and go, "Baa, baa," it be so fun to white-stone whizz.

But here comes Him Tiger. *"Grumma! Grum!"* Nearer and nearer, too. *"Grum! Grum!"* Louder and louder.

Sana Goat hurries her kids and runs off into the bushes.

Now you see, Anansi, he's still on the other side of the river, on the side with Him Tiger. He can't throw he-self across. And here come Him Tiger, just a-*grumma-grumming. "I'm going eat you, fella, Anansi!"* roars Him.

Just as Him is about to eat magic spider, Anansi, Anansi throws

a long, silver line across the river. It be just like a thin, line-bridge in the hot sun.

Anansi skittles and slides across his own silver spider thread. And he gets he-self clean away.

Him Tiger paws the thread down. Him, there, swishing his great, long tail. Stares across the water. And mean, fur all high up. And Him Tiger still growling, but not so loud now: *"Grumma. Grum! Grum!"* Because he couldn't catch anybody.

Walk about the bend. And there stands this story end.

CUNNIE ANANSI DOES SOME GOOD

ONCE, A LONG TIME AGO, a hungry-time be coming. So Cunnie Anansi and Sima Tiger go in search of food. Looking in grasses and bush, ah, no, they find nothing to eat. They do come upon a friend, Breda Parrot. They greet him, "Ah, yah, Brother!"

Quick! Cunnie Anansi, he has a thought. "We need new names. And we can take palm leaves to cover our eyes and mouths. See, by changing our names and hiding our faces, we can take anybody's food. And nobody will know it's us doing it."

"Ahhh!" say Sima Tiger and Breda Parrot.

Cunnie Anansi tells them, "I'm changing my name to Cherebanji."

"I'm changing my name to . . . Lukizaner!" Sima Tiger says.

Breda Parrot, him say, "I'm changing my name to. . . Greencornharo!"

"Come soon-time, we can take food from anybody!" Cunnie Anansi says.

"Come soon-time, we eat some food, put some away," agrees Sima.

"Time now, we eat some food, save some for a better day!" says Breda.

"Every house we come to, they have to tell us our new names," says Cunnie Anansi.

"And if not?" asks Sima.
"Then we take their food. We tie'um
and heave'um up a tree."
"Good news! *Good* news!"
roars Sima Tiger.
All three sing as
they go along:

*"Anansi be named
Cherebanji! Tiger be named
Lukizaner! Parrot be named
Greencornharo!"*

But bad luck-time is down the road. They come to Breda Parrot's house. "Knock! Knock!" Tiger paws the door. Mum Parrot comes out. She yelps surprise, so glad to see some company.

"And what be this bird's name?" Sima says to Breda's mum, and he looks at Greencornharo.

"Why, I'd know my son, Breda Parrot, anywhere!" Mum says.

"No, Mum!" cries Breda.

Too late! Sima Tiger and Cunnie Spider take hold of Mum Parrot's wings and tie her with long-grass blades. They vine-wrap her, hoist her high in a tree. She's squawking every which way.

"Let's take all her food," Cunnie Spider says. "Birdseed, and small winged things, too." An'en they eat'um all up.

Just then, Cunnie Anansi has a second thought, him. Says, "My brothers, excuse me. I must run home, get my umbrella. I'm afraid it might rain!" He runs off as quick as he can go. At home,

Anansi calls out:
"Mutha! Mutha!
Tiger and Parrot
coming to
get you!
I got a new
name, called
Cherebanji,
not Anansi.
Now what
is my name,
Mutha?"

And Mutha says, "Che-re-banji, my son! Not Anansi!"

"Good, Mutha! Now I have to hurry back to my friends!"

Cunnie Anansi runs back. Parrot asks where be his umbrella.

"Well, do you see some rain?" asks Cunnie Anansi. "When I got home, I decided it won't rain just yet."

The three friends go off singing:

"Anansi be
Cherebanji! Tiger be
Lukizaner! Parrot be
Greencornharo!"

Hungry-time make for fast friends and foul play. Bad luck up the road again. Here comes Sima Tiger's house. Breda Parrot pecks at the door: "Bika, bika!" The door opens; Mumma Tiger comes standing there.

"Mumma Tiger, what's this boy tiger's name?" asks Breda Parrot, flapping his wings to a flying beat.

"Why, that's my son, Sima Tiger. Wearing palm leaves—I'd know Sima anywhere!" says Mumma.

"Oh, no, Mumma!" Sima cries out. But too late.

Parrot and Anansi already tie her with grasses, so. Sima wraps her and hoists her up on the long vine. She, roaring all the way up. They take her boar meat store for their supper.

"Excuse me, friends," Cunnie Anansi says. "I must run home for seasoning of the wild boar meat." And off he runs home.

"Mutha!"
Anansi calls
his mama, strong.
"Mutha! Mutha!"
"Yes, my son?"
his mama says.
"Mutha, what's
my name?"
"Why, Cunnie Anansi,
my son!"
"No-o, Mutha,
my name be changed!
I be Cherebanji now!"
"Oh, all right,
my son,
Cherebanji."

Next, Anansi picks some pimientos and peppers for the wild boar meat. He runs to his mutha, says, "What's my name?" And she says, "Anan . . . I mean, Cherebanji!" And he warns her, "Don't forget, Mutha!" She tell'um, says, "I will not forget."

Cunnie Anansi goes in a hurry back to his friends. He sprinkles some pimientos and cut-up peppers on the boar meat. Two-them do eat yum-some. Breda thinks about it, but Parrot decides to stay with the seeds from Mum Parrot's house.

An'en, down the road they go, singing:

> *"Anansi be*
> *Cherebanji! Sima be*
> *Lukizaner! Breda be*
> *Greencornharo!"*

There's a great lot of bad luck this day. Next house they come to is Cunnie Anansi's house. For true! And Sima and Breda blow on the door. There be Mutha Spider.

Both Sima and Breda ask her: "Whose son be him with us?"

Mutha Anansi tell'um true: "Son be my own . . . Cherebanji!"

And they cannot tie her. And they are angry! They cannot vine-wrap her up a tree!

Cunnie Anansi hurries, takes Mutha Spider way far up a cotton tree. And there they stay. Until Mutha Spider makes a silk basket for to let Anansi down on the vine.

Anansi goes down, digs for yams. When he comes back, he's got nothing, but he sings sweetness, anyhow:

"Mutha, Mutha,
here be Anansi.
I want me
come up the tree!"

Next thing, Mutha Spider lowers the basket, and Anansi climbs in. She pulls him all the way up the cotton tree. Sima Tiger and Breda Parrot do watch all what is going on, and they don't like it at all. One day, they stand at tree-bottom, and both sing out:

"Mutha, here be
your boy, Anansi.
Sure him need come
upside there!"

"My son, what makes your voice sound double?" Mutha calls.

"Oh, Mutha, I catch the cold."

Mutha Spider lets down her basket. Both Sima and Breda get in. Mutha pull'um and pull'um. But they be so heavy, she can't pull'um fast. She bawls, "Son, what makes you sooo heavy?"

Says Breda Parrot, "Oh, Mutha, I eat such a lot of—"

Just then, there comes Cunnie Anansi! Him sees Mutha Spider pulling up Tiger and Parrot. Anansi hollers, "Mutha, let drop the basket!"

"What's that you say, my son? You want the basket?"

"No-o! No-o! Let it drop, Mutha. It's Tiger and Parrot riding!"

Mutha Spider drops the basket like it is red hot. Tiger and Parrot fall down hard. Sima breaks his leg. Parrot wrenches his wing. They whine and squawk like two babies.

"Help! Please, Mutha Spider, I hurting!" cries Sima.

"I hurting worse, Mutha Spider," Breda yelps.

"I'll mend you both, if you will be good," says Mutha. "Let your mamas down, and they can scold you and switch you."

“We’ll let’um down! We’ll be good!” Sima and Breda promise, so.

“All right, then,” says Mutha Spider. And she comes down in the basket. She mends them, gets some palm oil and leaf, and fixes them, wing and foot. “You promise. You will eat only what you find or ask for? You won’t take?” Mutha Spider asks.

They mumble uh-huh, they promise, looking sheepish at Anansi. “Friend, Anansi!” they exclaim.

“Don’t you try to get my Anansi back,” Mutha Spider tells them.

“And why, so?” asks Anansi. “Because, Cunnie Anansi is wiser than Parrot is flyer, smarter than Tiger is strong!”

TRICKSTERS—AFRICAN

THIS SECTION INTRODUCES sly, spindly, and crafty Spider, a leading animal trickster of West African countries—Ghana, Liberia, and Sierra Leone. We also meet the animal trickster Hare, of Bantu-speaking East, Central, and South Africa and western Sudan. There are other tricksters, too, and one is the little-known Cunnie Rabbit in a tale from Sierra Leone. The origin of Cunnie Rabbit's name has long been a subject of mystery and speculation (see "The Story Ring of Trickster Tales," page 10). In the tale "Cunnie Rabbit and Spider Make a Match," the two grand tricksters have a wrestling battle royal, in which they display some of their magic. The other animals in this tale are not cast just as onlookers, but they take turns in the match as well. There is a universal and timeless quality to this tale, for it goes beyond trickery into the realm of godlike supernatural power.

In other tales, humorous yet often pardonable tricks are played on the unsuspecting. This gives rise to the sense that the animal tricksters were invented by the community to cast away acts of human misbehavior from more suitable deeds. These animal characters first walked and talked and performed outlandish tricks because the people needed them to. We're glad they did. They amuse us with their tricks, even when they escape punishment. They seem very human, very much like ourselves.

The language in the African section may seem more complex. Actually it is a more formal sounding translation. The infinitive "to be" construction harks back to the early translations into English.

CUNNIE RABBIT AND SPIDER MAKE A MATCH

In this African tale, Cunnie Rabbit is not a rabbit at all. He is a "water deerlet," a small gazelle.

LONG TIME WAS, they called the animals in the forest, *the beef.* Sun hot, they say it bleached the beef almost white from the day they were born there.

The beef had no water, nothing. The country be bone dry. So the beef, they come together in a place to talk over what to do about it. And from the big beef elephant to the little one spider, they all study how to fix this one gre-e-at bad trouble.

Now Cunnie Rabbit, the deerlet, always stays apart but close enough to hear. He says not a word. He looken just like he-self, and he can do about anything. He listen to what all-them say. And he be thinking, "What must I do to get water?"

By and by, Cunnie Rabbit, him, runs home. There, he start'um dig down. He dig and *dig* down. For what? Him rabbit is digging for a well, what for! Water comes soon, and he drinks he-self cool, way down inside him.

All the beef sniff the well water on the air. They come, following the sweetness scent. Every one-them runs over to Cunnie Rabbit's house.

"Friend!" one beef says. "We have nothing to drink. If we don't get water, we're going to fall down! Give us some water!"

Cunnie Rabbit, him, says: "The one tell'um me to give water, tell'um him to come make a match. Come wrestle!"

Mister Spider, him, the one. And he says: "All right, then."

Now Spider and Cunnie Rabbit make the match.

First match, Cunnie Rabbit lifts Spider up to the sky. Spider comes down hard, he hits flat on the ground. Mister Spider, he

gets up, brushes his legs. An'en, he raises Cunnie Rabbit up. See, this beef is different from today. This beef can do anything.

Cunnie Rabbit, him goes up to the sky. Up there, he holds him a horn. Why so? 'Cause he can! He can-do and be-do Cunnie Rabbit. He have it all, can-do all.

He blows the horn, and the dark comes down. He blows it again, and down comes dayclean. An'en, he falls down next and takes him hold of the earth—*whoomp*! But Cunnie Rabbit, him, get'um back up!

Second match, Rabbit raises Mister Spider up way high. For one rainy season and one dry season, Spider, him, stays on top of the sky. "Ee! Ee!" Spider cry. And he fall'um back down. He says, "Friend, Cunnie Rabbit, I can't do it. You wrestle too hard. You are the strongest one!"

Then all the beef take turns. They try and try, but none can best lee-lee ole Cunnie Rabbit.

The big beef, Elephant, comes. Says, "Where's this one says he's most strong? Let'um come on, make the match. I need some water now!"

Cunnie Rabbit comes outside. He boasts, "Me! I, the strongest!"

Big Elephant! Big, fat beef! Before Cunnie Rabbit knows it, Elephant has his long snout out straight. He wraps Cunnie Rabbit in it and flings him. He turns, turns, turns him and lifts him up, way up. He *jams* Cunnie Rabbit to the sky!

An'en, Cunnie Rabbit gets he-self loose to the ground. He holds the elephant and raises up that beef.

"You be so little," Elephant says, "how you do me so high?"

Elephant falls down; he so heavy he breaks up the ground. He grabs Cunnie Rabbit one more time, too. Elephant wraps his long snout around him and drags him, and he pins him down.

The match goes rough. Going round and round, them, grabbing and pulling, pitching and flinging. The place where they wrestle grows big and wide as Freetown. The ground goes warm, and the whole place catches afire. Large-as-Freetown place burns so long, only the sand be left. And ashes. Ashes rise on the wind and fall on all the beef and everything.

All the beef pay no mind to ashes. They watch the match. Long time passes. But Elephant never wins over Cunnie Rabbit. The beef, they bow to him, Cunnie Rabbit. Each clasps his own hands. "*Do*," each says, "give us water. We'll give you all we got."

Cunnie Rabbit says, "All right. Each beef must drink one cup of water."

But the bargain was this-a-way. If a beef won't drink all the cup, he must give Cunnie Rabbit one piece of cloth. "You must say," Cunnie Rabbit tell'um, " 'this cloth be for the water I waste.' "

The cup was great big! Bigger than Freetown, England, and 'Merica.

Elephant, him, says: "I take the first drink." He takes the cup. He puts his long mouth inside it. He draw'um, draw'um, until he done'um.

All the beef drink, and all done'um. (Long time ago, the beef can drink a giant cup.) Next thing, they have all the water spread out, and they fire-cook rice in a pot big as the whole town. Yes! They eat the rice. All, elephant to spider, sheep to goat, they eat the rice. Wide water spreads upon them.

Well, they must swim. In the water, ashes from the large-as-Freetown fire melt. The beef, once all white, are white no more. Some now come red; some, brown. There's beef come black, and some make spot-and-spot, and stripe. And so until today—ashes make them all kinds of colors, stripes, and spots.

One time, when one little goat been begging for some water, Cunnie Rabbit says, "Call your mama, her, to come here and get you some water."

And little goat calls, "Ma-aaa, Ma-aaa!" And goat say, "Ma-aaa, Ma-aaa" until this day. Mebbe one day, big beef will pass by Cunnie Rabbit for strength. But forever and for true, Cunnie Rabbit pass all them beef—not for strength but for sense.

Cunnie Rabbit be king!

FREETOWN

HOW CHAMELEON BECAME A RIDE

ONE TIME, not my time, and not your time, it was a time for these three beef. Spider, Lizard, and Chameleon wanted to go see Freetown. But they had no boat to carry them there. So they were standing by the water, talking close.

"One-us has to be the boat," said Lizard.

"Can't be me, I'm all over legs!" Spider declared.

"You're too spindly," agreed Lizard. "It must be you, Chameleon. You're the biggest, and the one-us that most favors a boat."

"I see that!" said the spider. "You look right like one, Chameleon! Your hands'll be the oarlocks. Your tail'll be much like the rudder. And with your head as the bow, we'll place what load we carry at that inside part."

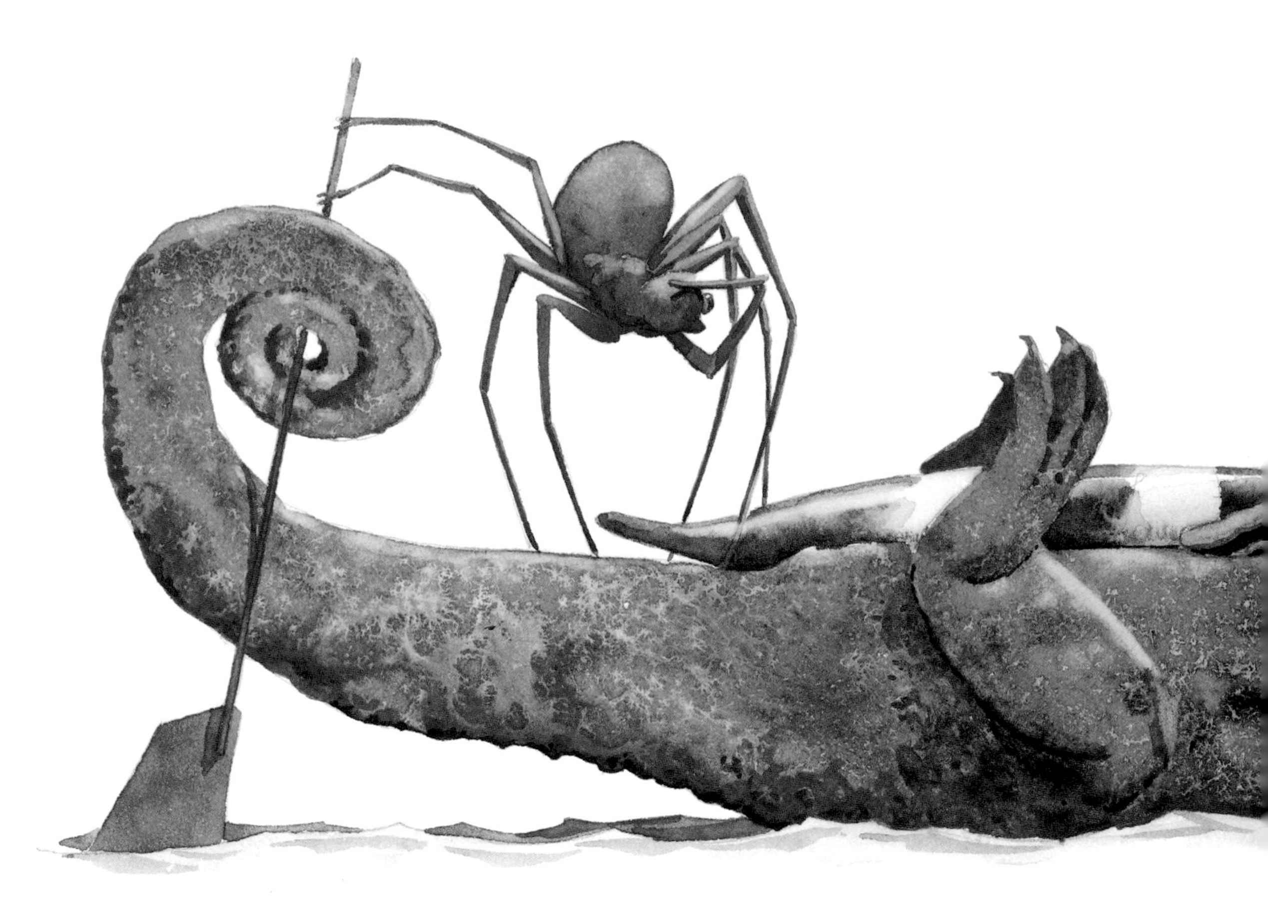

"I see," said Chameleon. He did see, and directly, he said, "I agree. I'll be the boat. I'll turn over, me, and lay my back down flat. Brothers, you'll sit down on me like you sit in any boat prow."

"All right!" said the spider.

He and Lizard climbed on top of this boat, Chameleon.

"Lizard, you take the oars," Chameleon ordered. "Put them through my hands." He had but two fingers and a thumb on each hand.

The lizard put the oars through Chameleon's hands, now held like oarlocks. He pulled the oars through the water. They began to go.

"I'm the captain!" Spider announced, sitting up there on Chameleon's curled tail. He held a steering stick.

"I'm the boatman," said Lizard. "I can pull hard with my feet!"

"And I'm the boat," said Chameleon. "It'll be all right for a while."

They came to a place where stones and rapids broke up the water. Captain Spider steered the bouncing boat against the stones. Just for devilment, he did. He kept doing it, jamming him-boat, Chameleon, on top of the stones. Chameleon soon got tired, and a little sore.

"Are we there, yet?" he asked. His head was back; his eyes were just above the waterline.

"No, Brother, we've come not halfway just yet," Spider answered. He steered the boat right near one big and heavy rock. At the same time, Lizard pulled hard on the oars.

Chameleon's back hit the rock, and he sat partway up and hollered, "Whoo-wee-ee! Friend, I don't like the tricky way you are doing me today!"

Spider made like he was sorry, saying, "Oh, friend, hush yah!" as kindly as he knew how. He did, for true! The boat, Chameleon, lay back down. The lizard was pulling, pulling, long time, pulling through the water. Until Chameleon got too tired, him, and asked, "We reached Freetown yet? Why is it so far?"

Said the spider, "Not so far no more. Look, yondro is the town."

"Didn't ask you that," said the chameleon. "I asked: Are we there yet?"

Spider said, "No, but there 'tis, over yondro."

"Friend, Spider, I don't like any trick, you hear? Tell me now if we've reached the place!"

But Spider said the same. "It just be yondro, Brother!"

"That's it," Chameleon said, way upset, too. "I'm coming out. You-all best swim yourselves to town."

"Oh, no. Oh, no," said the spider. He begged and begged.

Until Chameleon changed his mind. "All right. All right." And they went and they went until they come close to the land. Then Chameleon asked, "We done reach?"

Spider said, "Yes."

"I can turn over?" asked Chameleon.

"Not yet," Lizard tell'um. "We got to get all the way to shore."

When they got all the way to shore, Spider tell'um, "Now turn over. We reached Freetown!"

This be so. You see how him Chameleon do walk? He lifts one foot and then the other—not so fast because Spider jammed him on top of the stones and rock. That hurt his feet and back. And until this day, it makes Chameleon shake the pain out and take one slow step at a time.

OLD MISTER TURTLE GETS A WHIPPING

ONE TIME, not my time, but someone's time, Mister Turtle was out crawling close to Leopard's house. He spied Leopard's missus standing there in the door-mouth.

Old Turtle bowed 'n said, "How do, ma'am?"

"Thank you, I'm well," the missus tells him. "How's yourself, Mister Turtle?"

"Well," Turtle said, "this time, the fever is walking with me, and my skin hurts me all over. I'm so sick with fever, I'm a-go to the bush for roots. I'll make a root tea."

"That sounds proper," says Missus Leopard.

"By the way, ma'am, where might Mister Leopard be today?" asked Old Mister Turtle.

"Out hunting, him," says the missus. "You haven't seen him?"

"No, ma'am," Turtle replied. "So sorry he's away far. Because surely if he be here, I'd go ride him like a horse."

"Oh, no!" says the missus, shocked. "You couldn't ride'um Mister Leopard like a horse!"

Seeing how he'd upset the missus, Mister Turtle left. And when Mister Leopard come on home, Missus tell'um, "Turtle come by here. Says he going to ride you like a horse!"

"He say what?"

"That's what Turtle says. He's going to horseback ride you."

Well, Mister Leopard went wild. He cracked his teeth. He growled. He made tracks over to Turtle's house. He tell'um so: "You say you will ride me like a horse!"

"Not me!" says Old Mister Turtle. "I never said nothing like that!"

Leopard says, "All right, then, let's go ask the missus."

Mister Turtle says, sounding pitiful, too, "I can't walk, Bruh. I am sick with fever all on me."

"Come, I'll tote you," Leopard tell'um.

And Old Mister Turtle, he says right back, "Fever will make me fall, Bruh. Get me a little rope. I'll tie it around your mouth, Mister Leopard. I'll hold on to the rope so when I shake with the fevers, I won't fall off you."

Leopard got him the rope.

An'en, Turtle says, "Give me one little stick, Mister Leopard, so I can keep the flies from bothering us both."

Leopard got him a stick. And then they go, with Leopard carrying Mister Turtle. Galopidy, galopidy, go. And Turtle bounced up there, holding the rope. He flogged Mister Leopard with the stick, just like somebody riding a horse would do.

When they reached Leopard's house, his missus was waiting. She pointed at Mister Leopard, tell'um, "Well, 'tis true! Turtle say he's going to ride you like a horse. And he's riding you, for true!" She's laughing so!

Mister Leopard grabbed Old Mister Turtle down from off his back. Mister Leopard, him mad now.

Leopard takes the rope away. Takes the stick out of Turtle's

claw. He holds
Mister Turtle tight. And he
finds a great, bigger stick. He gives
Old Turtle a flogging he will not soon forget. And he
flogs him until Turtle's hard back shell is cut and cut all over it.

So you see, that's the story told sometime. Old Mister Turtle did ride Mister Leopard like a horse. And still today, the marks of the turtle-whipping be right there on top of Old Mister Turtle's back.

There's no denying what you can plainly see, now is there?

THE ANIMALS SHARE

KING LION called all the animals together. "No rain falls," he told them. "The lakes are dry. There is no water for you. So you must dig a well."

The animals grumbled until King Lion swished his tail for silence.

King Lion roared, "All must do their part and take their turn!"

But Shulo, the hare, said to himself, "I won't waste my time digging. Let the others do it." He ran off by himself.

All the other animals gathered to do their share. They came from all over the country. And they danced as they trotted to the place chosen for the well. They thought by dancing they would kick up the ground. And that would be their way of digging.

The animals lined up, singing, one by one:

"I'm coming, joggy-jog trot
kuputu, kuputu
the dirt is flying!"

Njou Elephant danced and sang, said:

"I give my place to you,
Nyati Buffalo!"

Nyati danced, then gave his place to Shelen, the bush-buck. And so it went, until all had sung and danced. But no seeping wet came. There was no water anywhere.

But then, see, the animals thought they had been digging. Yet their dancing had only packed the earth down harder. So they had a meeting. King Lion called on Hamba, the tortoise. Hamba was old and very wise.

"The water is *inside* the earth," Hamba said. And he dug down far beneath, far into the ground. There, he found water!

All the animals were happy. King Lion was very much pleased. But he knew they could not trust Shulo, the hare. "Shulo has done nothing," King Lion said. "But we know he will come in the night to take some water. Each night, one of you must watch the well."

Bongo, the hyena, spoke out. "I will watch the first night."

Of course, Shulo was already planning how he could take the water.

He filled his calabash with honey and went to the well. There, he spied Bongo. Shulo started talking to himself: "My calabash is full of something so sweet, anybody who tastes it won't get a second taste unless he's tied up."

"Ho, Shulo!" said Bongo. "Give me a taste of the sweets in your calabash."

Shulo dipped a stick in the calabash and smeared just a little honey across Bongo's lips.

Bongo licked his jaws. "More!" he cried. "Tie me up, Shulo, for I must have a second taste."

So Shulo tied up Bongo, front and hind feet. He gave no second taste. Instead, he went to the well and drank all he wanted. He filled his water gourds. He jumped in the water and splashed around. And he left the well muddy and dirty.

All the animals took their turns, and it happened every night that each one was tricked by Shulo, the hare. He carried full water gourds home. And through the long drought, his family had plenty to drink.

At last, it was Hamba Tortoise's turn to watch by the well. Hamba went down in the water and lay quietly on the bottom.

"So they've all given up!" laughed Shulo, when he came to the well and found no one there. "This well is mine without any digging!" He put his gourds down and jumped into the water.

But something caught at Shulo's foot. Next, something held him tight so he could not get away.

What a fix Shulo was in! He said, "Is that you, Hamba? I know it is! I've got something for you that's so very sweet. I'll let you have a taste." Shulo hoped Hamba would open his mouth.

Hamba never said a word. He held Shulo until daylight came. When all of the animals came to the well to drink, there was Shulo, caught at last. The animals seized Shulo and took him to King Lion. "You would not help to dig the well," said King Lion. "You stole the well water and made the well all muddy. You must not live another day!"

"Oh, no!" cried Shulo. "Oh, my great king! If I must die, let me sing one song, let me dance one dance!"

"There can be no harm in that,"
King Lion thought. He was merciful
and granted Shulo his wish.
The hare began to clap his hands.
He danced and sang:

"You, oh hare,
going away.
Returning when?
Tomorrow!"

All the animals began to beat time
to the music. They clapped and sang
with Shulo, his song was so delightful.
Soon they stomped their feet in the dance.
And in a little while, dust rose up
from the dry earth and made
a thick cloud around them.
Long time, when tired out,
the animals stopped and lay down.
A fine dance! They couldn't see one another
for the dust. And when it cleared?
Where was Shulo, the hare?
Gone, long gone, with his gourds all full.
No one, not even King Lion,
knows where he went.
Or if he will return—tomorrow!

ABOUT THESE TALES

LONG AGO, the tellers who made up these stories took traits of bad behavior found among their neighbors and other acquaintances and combined them with a certain wit and bold attitude in tales of animal practical jokesters. Adding to the listeners' and readers' general hilarity is the bewilderment of the animal trickees. These victims, such as Wolf and Gator, seldom realized until too late that they'd been bamboozled. In this section, I give further explanation about the fascinating animal tricksters in this book.

TRICKSTERS—AMERICAN

BUH RABBY AND BRUH GATOR, page 15

In "Buh Rabby and Bruh Gator," the alligator is outwitted by that grand old trickster, Buh Rabby. Buh is an early form of Bruh or Brer (Brother). Rabby is a colloquial name for the rabbit trickster in early animal stories of the Plantation Era.

The alligator in its natural habitat is never found very far inland. Therefore, it is often a part of coastal folktales. However, in such stories the alligator rarely gets the chance to play the fiddle, while the rabbit, often depicted as a fiddler, or the frog, are around. This is an elaborate *pourquoi*, or why-and-how, tale, giving reasons for the alligator's appearance and how he learned about trouble, a popular combination in many stories. There is no curved, bony ridge in front of the eyes of the American alligator, although there is such a ridge in spectacled caiman, another swamp species of alligator.

Buzzard and Wren Have a Race, page 25

It's been said that the trickster takes away the happy ending from those who think too highly of themselves. In this case, it's the high-flying buzzard who the tiny trickster gets the best of. "Buzzard and Wren Have a Race" is a flying contest tale that is won by deception. It has many versions, going back to Grimms' fairy tales. Bruh Wren saves the fun of it for all who hear his tale.

Buzzards are rarely tricksters, although in this story, the buzzard wants to have some fun with Wren. Perhaps buzzards are seen as too scary-looking. In one version of the story, the wren rides on Eagle's back, wins the contest, and becomes king. And here, the little bird does turn the trick quite well on the buzzard. This tale hails from Virginia and was told in an ordinary black vernacular.

The Cat and the Rat, page 33

This is a wonderful, short tale about three not-so-nice characters. "The Cat and the Rat" comes from the swamp region of Georgia. Collected in the late 1800s, such stories were often told before the Civil War. Here, the fox is the trickster. The larger, smarter animal outwits the dupes — Cat and Rat. The moral at the end places the tale in the realm of fable.

"The Cat and the Rat" was collected in the Gullah speech. The last paragraph beginning with "Never call in a bigger rogue. . . " would be written in Gullah as follows: "Wen tief plunder, better fuh dem share um mongst demself den trust ter call een bigger rogue fur dewide um."

Bruh Wolf and Bruh Rabbit Join Together, page 39

The wolf and the rabbit take their traditional folklore places in this story from the Sea Islands of South Carolina. Wolf is the stupid partner while Rabbit is the mischievous trickster. To African Americans of the Plantation Era, Bruh Rabbit was a hero. Small and apparently weak, Bruh Rabbit and his tales bolstered the oppressed slaves' dream of overcoming the so-called master. "Bruh Wolf and Bruh Rabbit Join Together" is a classic folktale of deception in which the clever trickster, ever polite and considerate, dupes his slow-witted victim.

TRICKSTERS—WEST INDIAN

That One, Anansi, page 47

In "That One, Anansi," the grand trickster is up to his usual tricks. Anansi often starts out in a cordial, polite manner, only to show his true, conniving self later on. After much twisting and turning, Anansi shows he can never be trusted.

The end rhyme to the story is not unusual. It is also quite common to open an Anansi escapade with some form of the age-old "Once upon a time." Our tale opens with, "Time was. . . . "

In the Caribbean islands of the West Indies, kitchens of plantation houses were separated from the house proper. This was often true in America, as well. The kitchen, made of stone, was to the side of the yard. Food travelled on covered trays, on the heads of servants, back and forth between the big house and the kitchen.

Magic Anansi, page 53

There is a curious mixture in "Magic Anansi," revealing how East Indian and African traditions come together to complement each other. The tiger is the magnificent cat of Asia. The Americas were never the natural habitat of tigers. Yet the influence is evident of the East Indian population, who brought their stories with them as they migrated to West Indian Islands.

Tigers are, of course, indigenous to areas from Siberia to Sumatra. The Bengal tiger is the well-known tiger of India. The most famous East Indian tiger story is the familiar tale of "Little Black Sambo," Sambo being originally an Indian boy. The boy easily became translated into an American black child as East Indian immigrants settled in the predominantly black islands of the Caribbean. And as a stereotype that fit well with the white planter image of "subservient" blacks, "Little Black Sambo" has been, for generations, quite unpopular with African Americans.

So it happens that East Indian tigers, West Indian and African spiders, and American and African goats become part of the same story and ever popular in countless other tales.

At first, it appears that Him Tiger is going to beat out both Anansi and Sana Goat. But Anansi uses his magic, which he keeps to himself most of the time, until he needs it. Willful magic is a useful folktale mechanism! Rather than trickery, in this tale Anansi combines magic with a natural spider phenomenon, the spider silk thread. Thus, magic Anansi saves not only Sana Goat and her kids, but himself as well.

CUNNIE ANANSI DOES SOME GOOD, page 59

This tale and others like it were called a "contribution from West Indian Negroes" when they were first published in 1899, and they were thought to be in the same class with stories about the American Bruh Rabbit. Yet the original tale, modified here, had a much more violent turn.

The illustrations from the original publication reflect East Indian people rather than West Indian. But the tales are told in the same Gullah-sounding speech that at one time pervaded all of the American South: " 'What you say my son? You want debushel basket?' An' him say: 'Noa, let dem dwop, dwop! It's Tiger and Paarat!' " The collector, who was from Jamaica, had then recently moved to America.

Cunnie means cunning. In this version, revised by the author, Anansi saves his mother. The other two mothers are also saved. In the original, Sima and Breda don't fare so well: "Tiger and Paarat break dey necks, an' den Annancy and him mumma. . . eat dem." The moral at the end reads: "Cunny — cunny better dan strong!" Meaning, cunning is better than strength.

There is a trace of "Rumpelstiltskin" in the guessing of names, which demonstrates how a powerful European fairy tale can widely influence stories in a variety of cultures.

TRICKSTERS—AFRICAN

CUNNIE RABBIT AND SPIDER MAKE A MATCH, page 75

In this tale, two great West African tricksters are in a wrestling match. Cunnie Rabbit, as the trickster is called, isn't a rabbit at all. He is a "deerlet," a very lee-lee (meaning little) African deer. In the illustration for the story, published in 1903, Cunnie Rabbit has hooves, a short white tail, and a glossy coat "of softest satin. . . a little creature."

The American Bruh Rabbit trickster may owe some of his style to the African Cunnie Rabbit. But Cunnie Rabbit is clearly the more powerful of the two. He wins over all the animals with his supernatural power; not even the elephant can overcome him. In other tales, Mister Spider surpasses all others for cunning. But in "Cunnie Rabbit and Spider Make a Match," Mister Spider's contribution to the story seems small. And he cannot beat Cunnie Rabbit for magic power or wisdom.

"Cunnie Rabbit and Spider Make a Match" is also a *pourquoi* tale, explaining how all the animals became different colors, with various designs on their coats.

"*Do*" is said with the gesture of cringing and bowing, as in a plea. Freetown is the largest city, the capital, of Sierra Leone, and its chief port. An additional note about Freetown: as mentioned in "A Note from the Author," an English abolitionist, Granville Sharp, selected the site south of the mouth of the Sierra Leone (Lion Mountains) River in 1787 as a haven for African slaves, freed and destitute in England. In 1791, the Sierra Leone Company assumed responsibility and helped settle slaves from Nova Scotia, from Jamaica, and from captured slave ships. Here we have the probable explanation of how Cunnie deerlet became a rabbit. More than likely, some of the former slaves who settled in Africa until the end of the American Civil War brought tales of Bruh Rabbit with them.

The last sentence of this story, written in the Gullah speech, reads: ". . . say he nar (is) king of de beas' fo'wise oh; not fo'stout, but fo'sense."

How Chameleon Became a Ride, page 85

Everything unusual needs to be explained, and many of these folktales tell why something came to be the way it is. Thus, a solution is offered for Chameleon's peculiar and slow gait. The explanation builds on Spider's trickery. He is the trickster in this tale and slyly causes "the boat," Chameleon, to be scraped on the rocks.

At the time "How Chameleon Becomes the Ride" was published in 1903, "Hush yah" or "as-yah" was said to be the strongest expression of sympathy in the Sierra Leone "dialect" — the Gullah speech in which it was recorded.

Old Mister Turtle Gets a Whipping, page 91

Turtle is the trickster in many West African folktales. He is slow and not particularly strong, but he makes up for his frailties by being very shrewd. In "Old Mister Turtle Gets a Whipping," he makes the swifter leopard his riding horse. However, at the end, Old Mister Turtle gets his comeuppance. The moral teaching is drawn from both Leopard and Turtle's defeat. The leopard is obliged to get even after his own wife laughs at him. The story is also a trickster-*pourquoi* one, explaining how the turtle's shell became marked. The marks prove, for all time, that he got what he deserved.

Other versions of this tale of deception have a tiger or fox as riding horse, and the trickster is a hare or rabbit. The *bush* is the African term used for any uncultivated land. *Door-mouth* is a doorway or entrance. *Crack he teeth* means a contemptuous, whistling inhalation.

THE ANIMALS SHARE, page 97

Shulo, the hare, in "The Animals Share," has the usual trickster characteristics of cleverness and deception. He is always trying to get something for nothing, and he succeeds. Although we find Shulo's antics humorous, we do not approve of what he does. There are clear cultural values at work here. In real life, people will not put up with someone like Shulo who wants his share while never doing his share of the work. However, we all know humans who sometimes get away with bad behavior. The cultural learning here is that we accept individual failings as only too human.

Kuputu has no meaning. It is said because it imitates the sound of animals' loping.

Perhaps Shulo wandered to America, where his cousin in trickery, Bruh Rabbit, resides! Bruh Rabbit had similar troubles, which landed him in the briar patch, free at last!

The paintings for

A Ring of Tricksters

were executed in transparent watercolor

on paper handmade at the Barcham Green Mills

in Maidstone, Kent, Great Britain,

for the Royal Watercolour Society.

The three text typefaces used are

Kennerly for the American tricksters,

Berkeley for the West Indian tricksters,

&

Goudy Oldstyle for the African tricksters.

All three types were designed by

Frederic W. Goudy.

The illustrator would like to especially thank

Heinrich Kley

&

Wilhelm Raulbach

for their work,

which the illustrator has

unabashedly and freely quoted.

Production supervision by Angela Biola

The book was designed by

Kathleen Westray

&

Barry Moser.